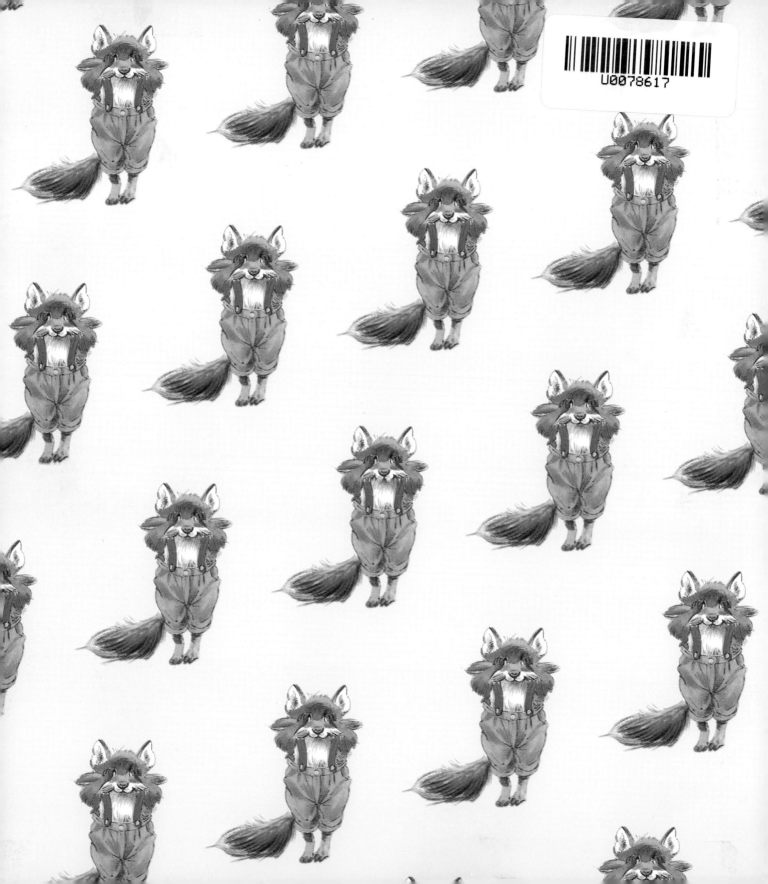

淘氣一族

Terry Dinning 著

Angela Kincaid 繪

陳培真 譯

三民書局

Read with Me Stories   ISBN 1 85854 749 0

Written by Terry Dinning and illustrated by Angela Kincaid

(Two stories: "Freddy Fox" and "Gilda the Witch")

First published in 1998

Under the title Read with Me Stories

by Brimax Books Limited

4/5 Studlands Park Ind. Estate,

Newmarket, Suffolk, CB8 7AU

My First Storybook   ISBN 1 85854 517 X

Illustrated by Angela Kincaid

(One story: "The Naughty Kitten")

First published in 1996

Under the title Read by Yourself

By Brimax Books Limited

4/5 Studlands Park Ind. Estate,

Newmarket, Suffolk, CB8 7AU

小狐狸弗瑞迪

Freddy Fox

"Do you want to go out to play with your friends, Freddy?" asks Freddy's mother.

"I do not want to go out because it is raining," says Freddy.

"Why not?" says Mrs **Fox**. She is **sewing** and wants some **peace** and **quiet**.

"I do not want to get my **tail** wet," says Freddy. He is very **proud** of his beautiful, red tail.

fox [fɑks]
名 狐狸

sew [so]
動 縫

peace [pis]
名 平靜

quiet [ˋkwaɪət]
名 安靜

tail [tel]
名 尾巴

proud [praud]
形 自豪的

「想不想和你的朋友出去玩呢？弗瑞迪？」弗瑞迪的媽媽問。
「我不想出去，正下著雨呢！」弗瑞迪說。
「為什麼不想呢？」狐狸媽媽說。她正在縫衣服，想要清靜一點兒。
「我不想把我的尾巴弄溼了呀！」弗瑞迪說。他對他那美麗的紅尾巴感到很自豪呢！

Outside Freddy sees his friend Desmond **Duck**. Desmond is **splashing** in the **stream**.

"Come and play!" he calls.

"I do not want to get my tail wet," calls Freddy.

"If you put your boots on and take an umbrella, you will not get wet," says Mrs Fox.

duck [dʌk]
名 鴨子

splash [splæʃ]
動 潑濺

stream [strim]
名 小溪

弗ㄈㄨˊ瑞ㄖㄨㄟˋ迪ㄉㄧˊ看ㄎㄢˋ見ㄐㄧㄢˋ他ㄊㄚ的ㄉㄜ˙朋ㄆㄥˊ友ㄧㄡˇ小ㄒㄧㄠˇ鴨ㄧㄚ子ㄗ˙戴ㄉㄞˋ斯ㄙ蒙ㄇㄥˊ在ㄗㄞˋ外ㄨㄞˋ面ㄇㄧㄢˋ。他ㄊㄚ正ㄓㄥˋ在ㄗㄞˋ小ㄒㄧㄠˇ溪ㄒㄧ裡ㄌㄧˇ戲ㄒㄧˋ水ㄕㄨㄟˇ玩ㄨㄢˊ耍ㄕㄨㄚˇ。
「過ㄍㄨㄛˋ來ㄌㄞˊ玩ㄨㄢˊ嘛ㄇㄚ˙！」小ㄒㄧㄠˇ鴨ㄧㄚ子ㄗ˙叫ㄐㄧㄠˋ喚ㄏㄨㄢˋ著ㄓㄜ˙。
「我ㄨㄛˇ才ㄘㄞˊ不ㄅㄨˋ想ㄒㄧㄤˇ弄ㄋㄨㄥˋ溼ㄕ我ㄨㄛˇ的ㄉㄜ˙尾ㄨㄟˇ巴ㄅㄚ呢ㄋㄜ˙！」弗ㄈㄨˊ瑞ㄖㄨㄟˋ迪ㄉㄧˊ大ㄉㄚˋ喊ㄏㄢˇ說ㄕㄨㄛ。
「如ㄖㄨˊ果ㄍㄨㄛˇ你ㄋㄧˇ穿ㄔㄨㄢ上ㄕㄤˋ靴ㄒㄩㄝ子ㄗ˙，拿ㄋㄚˊ把ㄅㄚˇ雨ㄩˇ傘ㄙㄢˇ，就ㄐㄧㄡˋ不ㄅㄨˋ會ㄏㄨㄟˋ弄ㄋㄨㄥˋ溼ㄕ了ㄌㄜ˙啦ㄌㄚ˙！」狐ㄏㄨˊ狸ㄌㄧˊ媽ㄇㄚ媽ㄇㄚ˙說ㄕㄨㄛ。

Freddy goes **upstairs** to **look for** his boots and his umbrella.

He looks under the bed. But they are not there. He looks in his **wardrobe**. But they are not there either.

Freddy hears his mother calling him. "Your boots and your umbrella are down here."

Freddy runs **downstairs** and is soon **ready** to go out to play.

upstairs [`ʌp`stɛrz]
副 朝樓上

look for
尋找

wardrobe
[`wɔrd‚rob]
名 衣櫥

downstairs
[`daʊn`stɛrz]
副 朝樓下

ready [`rɛdɪ]
形 準備好的

弗瑞迪上樓去找他的靴子和雨傘。
他看了看床底下，可是它們不在那兒。他往他的衣櫥裡頭瞧了瞧，可是它們也不在那兒。
弗瑞迪聽到媽媽喊他：「你的靴子和雨傘在樓下這裡啦！」
弗瑞迪衝到樓下，一會兒就穿戴整齊，準備出去玩了。

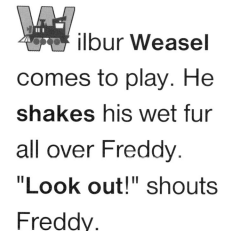

Wilbur **Weasel** comes to play. He **shakes** his wet fur all over Freddy.

"**Look out**!" shouts Freddy.

"Rain is **horrible**. What can we do?"

"Lots of things," says Desmond.

"First we can play a splashing game. We must find a big puddle, then **jump** in it as hard as we can. The biggest splash **wins**!"

weasel [`wizl]
名 黃鼠狼

shake [ʃek]
動 抖動

look out
小心

horrible [`hɔrəbl]
形 討厭的

jump [dʒʌmp]
動 跳

win [wɪn]
動 贏

黃鼠狼韋柏也來玩耍。他把溼答答的毛往弗瑞迪身上一甩。
「小心一點啊！」弗瑞迪大叫。
「下雨真討厭，我們可以做什麼呢？」
「很多事情啊！」戴斯蒙說。
「我們可以先玩踩水花的遊戲。我們找個大水坑，然後用全力跳進去，濺起水花最大的，便贏了囉！」

Everyone **chooses** a big puddle and jumps in it as hard as they can. **Splash**! Desmond makes a big splash. Splash! Wilbur makes a big splash. SPLASH! Freddy makes the biggest splash of all.

"This is fun," says Freddy.

"Excuse me," says a **voice** from high in the **branches** of a tree. "I don't think it is fun. You've made my **feathers** very wet."

choose [tʃuz]
📖 挑選

splash [splæʃ]
📖 噗通一聲

voice [vɔɪs]
📖 聲音

branch [bræntʃ]
📖 樹枝

feather [ˈfɛðɚ]
📖 羽毛

每個人都挑了個大水坑，使勁地跳進去。噗通一聲！戴斯蒙濺起了一個大水花。噗通一聲！韋柏濺起了一個大水花。噗通一聲！弗瑞迪濺起了最人的水花。

「真好玩！」弗瑞迪說。

「對不起，」從高處的樹枝上傳來一個聲音說。「我可不認為這樣子好玩呢！你們把我的羽毛全弄溼了啦！」

Olly Owl **flutters** his wet **wings**.
"Please stop that at once!" he **hoots**.
They all **scamper** away. Freddy's
tail is wet at the **tip**, but he does not **notice**.
"What shall we do now?" asks Freddy.
"I know," says Wilbur. "We can make some paper boats and **sail** them along the stream."

flutter [ˋflʌtɚ]
🎬 拍翅

wing [wɪŋ]
🎬 翅膀

hoot [hut]
🎬 呼呼叫

scamper [ˋskæmpɚ]
🎬 蹦跳

tip [tɪp]
🎬 尖端

notice [ˋnotɪs]
🎬 注意

sail [sel]
🎬 使（船）行駛

貓頭鷹歐力拍動他那溼答答的翅膀。
「請馬上停止！」他呼呼叫。
大夥兒一哄而散。弗瑞迪尾巴的末端溼了，可是他沒有注意到。
「現在我們該做些什麼呢？」弗瑞迪問。
「我知道。」韋柏說。「我們可以做些紙船，讓紙船沿著小溪航行啊！」

13

The paper boats **float** along the water.
"We can have a **race** with the boats," cries Desmond.
"Let's go!"
The three friends **cheer** their little boats along the stream. Freddy **drops** half his tail in the water, but he does not notice —his boat is winning the race! Desmond **swims** beside the boats. "Look at me," he calls. "I am **pretending** to be a yellow boat."

float [flot]
働 漂浮

race [res]
名 賽跑

cheer [tʃɪr]
働 為…加油打氣

drop [drɑp]
働 掉落

swim [swɪm]
働 游泳

pretend [prɪˋtɛnd]
働 假裝

紙船順水漂浮。
「我們可以和船賽跑。」戴斯蒙喊著。「出發！」
這三個朋友便沿著小溪跑了起來，替他們的小船加油。弗瑞迪的尾巴有一半垂到水裡，可是他沒有注意到——他的船就要贏得比賽了！戴斯蒙在船邊游來游去。「瞧瞧我呀！」他喊著。「我在假裝自己是一艘黃色的小船哩！」

15

"I wish we could all pretend to be boats," says Freddy. Then he has an **idea**. He takes his umbrella, **turns** it upside-down and sets it on the water. It floats just like a boat. He jumps into the umbrella. "I am the **captain** of this boat," he says.

Wilbur jumps in beside him.

Freddy's tail falls over the side and gets very wet, but he does not notice. He is too busy sailing his umbrella boat.

idea [aɪˈdiə]
名 點子

turn [tɝn]
動 翻轉

captain [ˈkæptn̩]
名 船長

「真希望我們都可以假裝自己是船。」弗瑞迪說。於是他有了一個點子。他把雨傘上下顛倒過來，放到水面上，傘就像船一樣地漂浮著。他跳進雨傘裡面。「我是這艘船的船長！」他說。

韋柏跳坐到他的旁邊。

弗瑞迪的尾巴掉出了傘邊，弄得溼漉漉的，可是他並沒有注意到，他正忙著駕駛他的雨傘船呢！

Then Desmond says,
"Time to go home.
Come on, everyone."
Desmond begins to
swim back up the stream.
He looks over his **shoulder**, but Freddy and
Wilbur are not behind him. They cannot make
the umbrella boat turn around. The stream is
carrying them **further** and further away!

shoulder [`ʃoldɚ]
名 肩膀

carry [`kærɪ]
動 帶走

further [`fɝðɚ]
副 更遠地

然後戴斯蒙說：「該回家囉！來吧！大夥兒！」
戴斯蒙開始往小溪的上游游回去。他轉過頭一看，發現弗瑞迪和韋柏並沒有跟在後頭。他們沒法兒讓雨傘船掉頭，溪水把他們愈沖愈遠了！

"Help us!" they cry.
Then Mrs Duck swims
along. She is looking
for Desmond. She
sees the umbrella

with Freddy and Wilbur in it and quickly
swims after it. She **pulls** it **safely** to the bank.
"Thank you," **gasps** Freddy.
He is **soaking** wet, but he does not notice —
he is too busy catching his **breath**!

pull [pʊl]
動 拉

safely [`seflɪ]
副 安全地

gasp [gæsp]
動 喘氣

soaking [`sokɪŋ]
副 溼透地

breath [brɛθ]
名 呼吸

「救命啊！」他們大叫起來。那時鴨媽媽
正一路游了過來，要尋找戴斯蒙。她看見
載著弗瑞迪和韋柏的雨傘船，便趕緊游
了過去，把船安全地拉到岸邊。
「謝謝！」弗瑞迪氣喘噓噓地說。
他渾身溼透了，可是他並沒有注意到——
他正忙著喘氣呢！

Everyone goes back to Freddy's house to dry in front of the **fire**. Soon, Freddy, Desmond and Wilbur are sitting in front of the fire drinking hot milk and eating cookies. **Suddenly** Freddy **remembers** his tail. "My **poor** tail," says Freddy.

fire [faɪr]
名 爐火

suddenly [`sʌdn̩lɪ]
副 突然地

remember
[rɪ`mɛmbɚ]
動 想起

poor [pʊr]
形 可憐的

大夥兒回到弗瑞迪家，在爐火前弄乾身子。不一會兒，弗瑞迪、戴斯蒙和韋柏便坐在爐火前喝起熱牛奶，吃起餅乾來了。突然間，弗瑞迪想起自己的尾巴。
「我可憐的尾巴！」弗瑞迪說。

"You must be very **careful** when you play near water," **scolds** Mrs Fox.

Mrs Duck has an idea.

"I will **teach** Freddy and Wilbur to swim like ducks," she says. "Then they can play safely in the stream."

"Now, Freddy," says Mrs Fox, "I have a **surprise** for you. **Close** your eyes."

Freddy closes his eyes.

careful [ˈkɛrfəl]
形 小心的

scold [skold]
動 責罵

teach [titʃ]
動 教

surprise [səˈpraɪz]
名 驚喜

close [kloz]
動 關，閉

「到水邊玩耍要要很小心的啊！」狐狸媽媽責罵著。

鴨媽媽有個主意。「我來教弗瑞迪和韋柏像鴨子一樣地游泳。」她說。「這樣他們就可以很安全地在溪水中玩耍了。」

「好了，弗瑞迪，」狐狸媽媽說，「我要給你一樣驚喜。眼睛閉上哦！」弗瑞迪閉起了眼睛。

"Now you can look," says Mrs Fox. She **shows** Freddy what she has been sewing. It is a **bright** yellow **raincoat**!

"You will look just like me," says Desmond.
"I will swim like a duck and look like a duck," **laughs** Freddy.

「現在你可以張開眼睛看了。」狐狸媽媽說。她給弗瑞迪看那個她一直在縫的東西，是一件鮮黃色的雨衣呢！
「你會看起來和我很像唷！」戴斯蒙說。
「我會游起來像隻鴨子，看起來也像隻鴨子呢！」弗瑞迪笑著說。

Say these words again.

friends	puddle
raining	feathers
beautiful	scamper
stream	sail
winning	yellow
stairs	shoulder
splashing	remembers

What can you see?

tail

umbrella

boots

paper boats

raincoat

救難小福星

Heather S Buchanan著　本局編輯部編譯
15×16cm／精裝／6冊

在金鳳花地這個地方，住著六個好朋友：兔子魯波、蝙蝠貝索、老鼠妙莉、
鼴鼠莫力、松鼠史康波、刺蝟韓莉，
他們遇上了什麼麻煩事？要如何解決難題呢？
好多好多精采有趣的歷險記，還有甜蜜溫馨的小插曲，
就讓這六隻可愛的小動物來告訴你吧！

 魯波的超級生日

 莫力的大災難

 貝索的紅睡襪

 史康波的披薩

 妙莉的大逃亡

 韓莉的感冒

老鼠妙莉被困在牛奶瓶了！糟糕的是，她只能在瓶子裡，看著朋友一個個經過卻沒發現她。有誰會來救她呢？
（摘自《妙莉的大逃亡》）

網際網路位址　http://www.sanmin.com.tw

© 小狐狸弗瑞迪

著作人　Terry Dinning
繪圖者　Angela Kincaid
譯　者　陳培真
發行人　劉振強
著作財　三民書局股份有限公司
產權人　臺北市復興北路三八六號
發行所　三民書局股份有限公司
　　　　地址／臺北市復興北路三八六號
　　　　電話／二五〇〇六六〇〇
　　　　郵撥／〇〇〇九九九八——五號
印刷所　三民書局股份有限公司
門市部　復北店／臺北市復興北路三八六號
　　　　重南店／臺北市重慶南路一段六十一號
初　版　中華民國八十八年十一月
編　號　S85538
定　價　新臺幣壹佰陸拾元整
行政院新聞局登記證局版臺業字第〇二〇〇號

ISBN　957-14-3087-0（精裝）